DEDICATION

I want to dedicate this book to my father, Clifford Lynn. He is my inspiration in life for all that I am. He taught me goodness, righteousness, and fairness, and I want to pass that on to my ten beautiful grandchildren. I love you to infinity, Dad.
I also want to acknowledge my incredible grandchildren that encouraged me to soldier on to finish my book. Thank you Wyatt, Josh, Brooklyn, Pierson, Preston, Riley, Jack, Avery, Lauren, and Luke. You make my heart smile every time I think of you. You are the loves of my life.
Martha Lynn

To order additional copies of this book, contact:
Xlibris LLC
1-888-795-4274
www.Xlibris.com
Orders@Xlibris.com

Joshy
And The
Giant
Goldfish

A FICTION CHILDRENS TALE

By Martha Lynn

Illustrations by Lyle John Jakosalem

INTRODUCTION

I was inspired to write this story with my grandson, Josh Michael Ramsey, when he was 4 years old. We went to the neighborhood pond many times to feed the large Koi fish. He always stood near the edge on a rock and I would hang onto him while he threw pieces of bread to the fish. One day out jumped the largest Gold Koi fish we had ever seen and tried to eat the bread right out of Josh's hand. We both never forgot that moment and promised to remember it forever for other children to enjoy. Thank you Josh, for all the joy, happiness, and love that you bring to me…Always and Forever,   Granny

Joshy and his parents live in Del Mar, California. He grew up around the ocean and they had a beautiful home that was in a cove backing up to an inlet to the water. He and his parents have always been boating, skiing, fishing and swimming and feeding the fish that come up to his favorite giant rock that juts out from the back yard overlooking the bay. He was so excited to leave the next day on their big sailboat for their family vacation.

Joshy and his parents were on a vacation in the tropical islands off the coast of Bora Bora. They had a big sailboat named Dreamscape and loved to travel. His dad, Reed and mom, Emma, were experienced sailors.

The sailboat was clipping along smoothly and they were having a great adventure when over the sunrise a big storm came up without warning. The sky turned very dark. The rain poured down sideways. Joshy was so scared. Emma told him to go below deck and lock himself in the galley and she and Reed would be there shortly. She told him that they loved him and not to worry that everything would be alright.

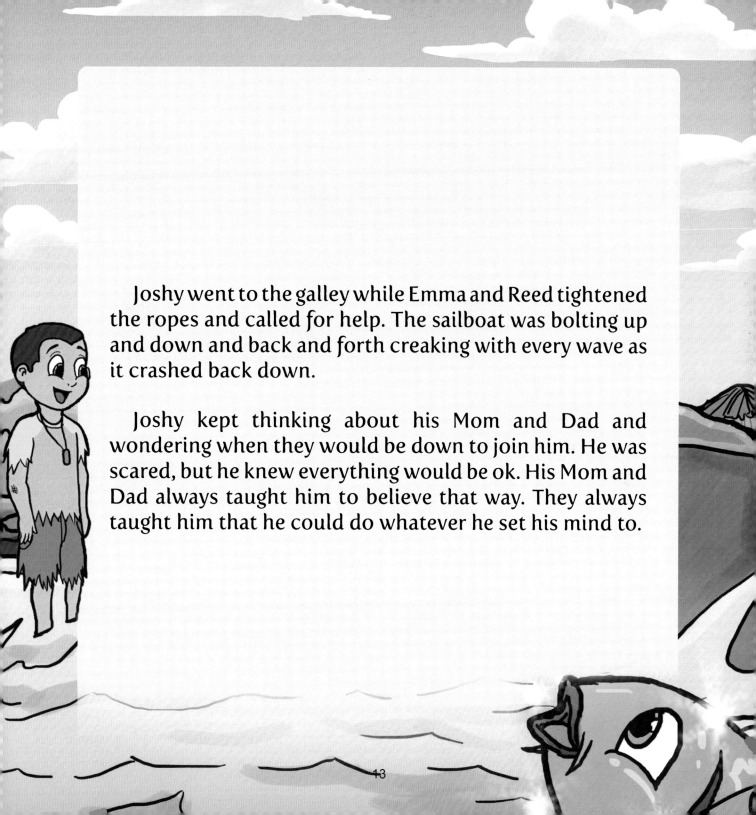

Joshy went to the galley while Emma and Reed tightened the ropes and called for help. The sailboat was bolting up and down and back and forth creaking with every wave as it crashed back down.

Joshy kept thinking about his Mom and Dad and wondering when they would be down to join him. He was scared, but he knew everything would be ok. His Mom and Dad always taught him to believe that way. They always taught him that he could do whatever he set his mind to.

All at once the boat lurched and then crashed against something very hard.....Joshy hung on tight as it crashed against the waves, the rain pounding against the wood. The Dreamscape was falling apart. He screamed out for his parents but no one replied.........Joshy collapsed and the world around him was silent except for the waves slapping against the broken rock and wood.

16

All of a sudden the sun was out and shining against the sand. Joshy woke up to find himself lying there covered in seaweed and debris, but he was alive and ok. He shouted for his Mom and Dad but no one was there.....He was all alone on what looked like a beach or small island. He was wet, hungry and wanted his mom and dad. Home seemed so far away and now he had to think about what to do.

He had never been by himself before. Mom had always made sure he had a nice warm bed, clean clothes, great home-made meals and everything he needed. Dad worked very hard to make sure that they had a nice home, great yard, and played ball and went fishing on his days off. He had never had to think about this before. Joshy began to cry. He felt like the whole world had gone away and left him here alone. "What am I going to do?" he cried.

Lucky for Joshy his Dad had taken him camping a lot and he knew how to look for some food. He didn't want to go too far into the jungle; after all, he was just a little boy. And another thing that bothered him...how did he get from the ocean to this shore? That was a mystery to him. Where were his parents? Were they alive? Were they looking for him? So many questions that he needed answers to ....Would he see them again? He couldn't think about this right now. First things first, he had to find food, and make a shelter as night would come soon.

Joshy made a bed of big green leaves and made a cover over his head with large palm leaves. He found some bananas and a coconut and a few berries and was able to crack the coconut enough to drink a little of the milk inside. Sleep came over him as the sounds of the jungle sang out through the night and all he dreamed of was finding his mom and dad and getting home.

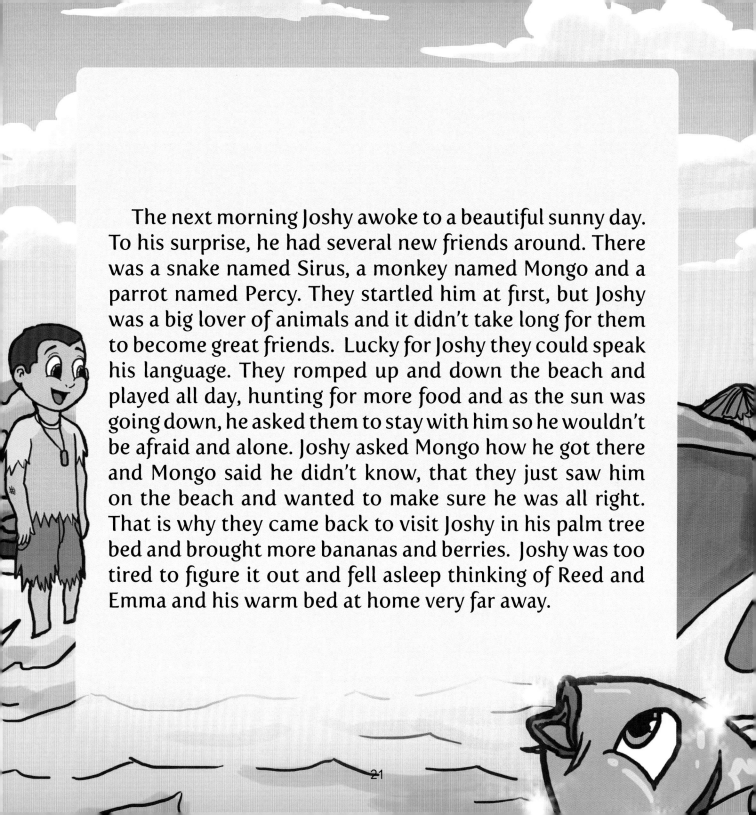

The next morning Joshy awoke to a beautiful sunny day. To his surprise, he had several new friends around. There was a snake named Sirus, a monkey named Mongo and a parrot named Percy. They startled him at first, but Joshy was a big lover of animals and it didn't take long for them to become great friends. Lucky for Joshy they could speak his language. They romped up and down the beach and played all day, hunting for more food and as the sun was going down, he asked them to stay with him so he wouldn't be afraid and alone. Joshy asked Mongo how he got there and Mongo said he didn't know, that they just saw him on the beach and wanted to make sure he was all right. That is why they came back to visit Joshy in his palm tree bed and brought more bananas and berries. Joshy was too tired to figure it out and fell asleep thinking of Reed and Emma and his warm bed at home very far away.

The next day Joshy decided to go fishing near the shore with his friends standing by. He made a spear out of bamboo and dove into the clear blue waters. Joshy was a great swimmer and could hold his breath for a long time. He saw all kinds of beautiful fish, coral, and reef. He caught a couple of fish and decided he had better go back to shore. As he was coming up out of the water, Joshy saw a shark off to his right. He was so scared as it was coming toward him and his prey fast. He knew he didn't have time to get to shore, then all of a sudden something large came up under him and pushed him out of the water and threw him onto the sand on the beach!!!! Joshy stood up just in time to see a huge Goldfish go back under the water and out of sight. He couldn't believe it, this giant Goldfish had saved his life!

Joshy knew he had to find out more. He found his friends and asked Mongo, Sirus, and Percy if they had ever seen this Giant Goldfish? They all seemed a little frightened and stammered around a bit. Well, said Percy, there is a tale that there is a magical Giant Goldfish in the waters that is bigger than any fish in the sea. It is from a magical kingdom of Koistana and protects the King and Queen and their palace there.

Her name is Kedialuna and is the protector of the sea. It is only a tale and has never been proven of course. Joshy knew that it was Kedialuna that had saved him and he wanted to meet this fish again.

The next morning Joshy went back to the shore and decided to go diving again. He dove deep into the blue waters with his friends waiting on shore. There was no sign of Kedialuna, so he went back to shore, disappointed at no sighting. Mongo and Percy were glad that he didn't find the Giant Fish this time as they were actually afraid. After everyone went to bed, Joshy sneaked out of his palm leaves and went to the shore again. He was sad and missing his parents and feeling hopeless that he would never go home.

Joshy sat on a huge stone that jutted out in the water crying. All of a sudden, Kedialuna popped up right there in front of him. Her beautiful Gold color glistened in the moonlight. Joshy wasn't afraid and reached out to touch her. He spoke to Kedialuna and asked why did you save me? Kedialuna nodded and replied that she was there to protect the good in the sea.

Joshy told her about the Dreamscape and his parents and Kedialuna listened intently nodding with every sentence Joshy spoke. She knew that Joshy's heart was heavy from being apart from his parents. She wanted to tell him the whole story, but it wasn't time yet. She had to gain his trust first. After Joshy finished his story about the shipwreck, Kedialuna asked him if he would like to go on an adventure under the sea. "Of course", he replied! "But how will I be able to breathe?" he asked. Kedialuna told him she had magical gills that he would develop and not to worry, that she had done this many times. So away they went, down into the sea, with Joshy on Kedialuna's side seeing the beautiful city of Koistana and the underwater plants, and animals. It was more beautiful than anything he had ever seen. Kedialuna helped him back to shore and Joshy went back to his palm leaf bed, exhausted, and fell fast asleep.

"Good Morning sleepy head", said Sirus. You have slept almost all morning! Are you OK? Oh yes, Joshy said. You won't believe what happened last night. Joshy began to tell Percy, Mongo, and Sirus about his underwater adventure and his friends were shocked. They wanted to believe, but they were still unsure, as this was considered folklore in their villages. They needed real proof that it was true. Joshy was disappointed, as he never told a lie. He told them he would prove that his story was true. They fished, hunted for berries, bananas, and coconuts and talked about other things until the sun went down.

After everyone went to sleep, Joshy went back to his large stone and waited again for Kedialuna. She arrived and they talked and Joshy told her about his friends and that they didn't believe him. Kedialuna knew that it was time to tell him about the Dreamscape and how she rescued him. Joshy, there is something you should know. During the big storm your parent's boat sank to the bottom of the ocean. The Coast Guard was able to rescue your parents; however, you were in the galley and couldn't get out. I heard your Mom and Dad screaming for you, so I followed the ship and rescued you and put you on the shore. Your Mom and Dad had already gone with the Coast Guard and flown away.

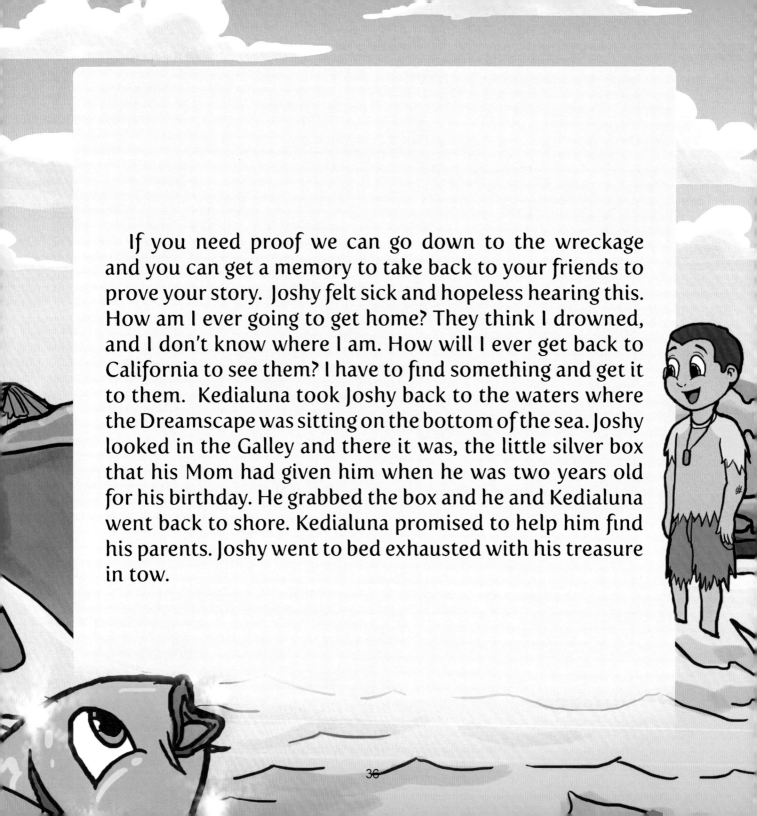

If you need proof we can go down to the wreckage and you can get a memory to take back to your friends to prove your story. Joshy felt sick and hopeless hearing this. How am I ever going to get home? They think I drowned, and I don't know where I am. How will I ever get back to California to see them? I have to find something and get it to them. Kedialuna took Joshy back to the waters where the Dreamscape was sitting on the bottom of the sea. Joshy looked in the Galley and there it was, the little silver box that his Mom had given him when he was two years old for his birthday. He grabbed the box and he and Kedialuna went back to shore. Kedialuna promised to help him find his parents. Joshy went to bed exhausted with his treasure in tow.

The next day was a beautiful sunny day. Joshy was up early to meet his friends. Mongo, Sirus, and Percy, I have something to show you all. I dove last night to the bottom of the ocean with Kedialuna again. I retrieved this silver box with my name on it from my parents when I was two years old and I take it everywhere. Now do you believe me? Oh my, said his friends! Kedialuna is real! And so is Koistana!

We are so sorry Joshy, that we didn't believe you! Tall tales and folklore are a part of our culture. What are you going to do now? We will help you any way we can! Kedialuna is going to help me too. Let's put our heads together and think of a plan. So all day long they thought about what might work to get Joshy home to Del Mar, California. Since he was on an Island there were no phones, no incoming boats, just natives that were not very friendly to strangers, so he had to figure this out with his friends Mongo, Sirus and Percy, and of course, Kedialuna. That night, they all decided to meet Kedialuna at the stone in the ocean.

Joshy, Mongo, Sirus, and Percy all went to the stone where Joshy knew that Kedialuna would be. Soon she arrived and met all of them. Joshy assured them that she was their friend, too. Kedialuna realized that she must help Joshy very soon as the natives drums could be heard in the near distance. This was troubling to his friends and to her and it was time to get their plan together. They decided to leave the next morning. It would be a long and dangerous trip and she wanted Joshy rested for the journey. He would need to say his goodbyes to his friends also. This made him sad, but he was more excited to see his parents soon and show them that he was alive and well. He could hardly wait. Kedialuna left and Joshy and his friends went back to their hiding place to eat a large meal of fruits and berries and spend their last night together.

It was dark now and the sky was beautiful and clear. Joshy could see stars dotting the sky everywhere he looked. All he could think about was going home, but there was sadness in his heart leaving the friends that had saved his life and been there for him. Joshy stood up and spoke to Mongo, Sirus and Percy. Friends, I can't thank you enough for all you have done for me. I love you like family and will think of you often when I leave tomorrow. You saved my life and I want to leave you something to remember me by when I am gone. He reached down and with tears in his eyes he handed them the silver box with his name on it and gave it to Mongo, Sirus, and Percy. Take care of this my friends, it is a very special gift and I cherish it with my heart. I will cherish you always in my heart, too. They all hugged and went to sleep. After all, good friends stay in your heart forever.

The sun rose bright and shining and Joshy was ready to go. Mongo, Sirus and Percy went to the big stone to see that he made it safely to the Ocean. Just like they planned, Kedialuna was there. Joshy hugged his friends and jumped into the Ocean waving to his friends as they disappeared under the deep blue waters. Just as before, Joshy developed the magic gills that Kedialuna gave him to breathe. She knew this would be a long and dangerous journey ahead.

They had been swimming for what seemed forever when a large school of hungry sharks came out of nowhere. Kedialuna could see the panic in Joshy's eyes and shook her head for him to relax. She had taken care of him before and would do it again. She circled around Joshy and then suddenly Kedialuna and Joshy were enclosed in a huge safety bubble that the sharks could not penetrate! The sharks banged into the sides over and over until they were exhausted and finally swam away. They continued to swim further and further toward California. Kedialuna decided to find a place to let Joshy rest, so she found a safe private beach area and they stopped for the night. Joshy was exhausted and fell asleep immediately on the warm sand thinking of home.

The next morning Joshy awoke and Kedialuna was there and they started their journey again. Joshy was excited as he knew they were almost home! They continued along seeing many beautiful fish in the deep blue waters. The coral was so many colors of peach, purple, pink and greens and he was so blessed to be able to see Nature's beauty in a way that no other person had been able to see with Kedialuna. He was the luckiest kid in the world to have this magical guardian looking out for him! All of a sudden they came upon a huge group of electric eels coming straight at them. Joshy was scared as he had never seen such a fierce looking group of underwater creatures! Kedialuna immediately created a tunnel for them through the middle of the eels and they swam right through the whole school of them and the family of jellyfish that was right behind them! Kedialuna had saved them again! She was magnificent and Joshy was astonished at her magical powers and thankful for them, too.

As Joshy and Kedialuna came around the bend of a marsh he got so excited! He recognized this very area! He had been swimming here all his life and it led right to his back yard and his favorite rock! He was almost home! Just a few more yards and he would see his parents again. Joshy was there! He touched the stone and climbed up on his rock! He was home! Kedialuna was right there by his side. He wanted to rush into the house, but he hesitated. There were things he needed to say to Kedialuna. He could see his parents in the family room watching TV. They looked so great! Joshy turned to Kedialuna and told her how much he loved her. He thanked her for saving his life several times and that he couldn't have lived without her. He wouldn't have seen his Mom and Dad without her, too. She just smiled and nodded, and nuzzled his chest. After all, it was her job to protect the Ocean and her Kingdom. Joshy told her that when he was a little boy that he used to feed the Koi goldfish with his Granny. When he was 4 yrs. old, they were out there and a Giant Goldfish jumped out of the water to eat the bread in his hand and he almost fell in the water! Kedialuna smiled a huge smile and winked and she said, " I know!" She jumped up and gave Joshy a great

big kiss on the cheek and with that Kedialuna disappeared into the water. Joshy knew then that Kedialuna had been taking care of him since he was a little boy! He smiled as the tears rolled down his face and he ran into the house yelling Mom, Dad, It is Joshy I am Home! They screamed for Joy and grabbed him and hugged him........Joshy...YOU ARE ALIVE! Joshy said YES! and you won't believe what happened and where I have been!

The End

Edwards Brothers Malloy
Oxnard, CA USA
November 7, 2013